Animal Fun

Written by Charlotte Raby
and Emily Guille-Marrett
Illustrated by Laszlo Veres

Collins

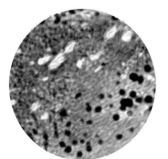
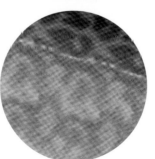

9

Where do these animals come from?

After reading

Letters and Sounds: Phase 1

Word count: 0

Curriculum links: Understanding the World: The World

Early Learning Goals: Listening and attention: children listen attentively in a range of situations; Understanding: answer 'how' and 'why' questions about experiences and in response to stories or events

Developing fluency

- Encourage your child to hold the book and to turn the pages.
- Look at each of the scenes together and encourage your child to talk about what they can spot. Ask them to describe each creature.

Phonic practice

- Look at pages 2–3 together. Say 'I can see a d-u-ck', sounding out all of the phonemes (letter sounds). Ask your child to point to the right animal. Then ask them to repeat the phonemes and blend them together 'd-u-ck, duck'.
- Do the same for the animals: sheep (*sh-ee-p*), chick (*ch-i-ck*).

Extending vocabulary

- Look at the different scenes together. Ask your child if they can tell you the names of the animals (or parts of animals) in the little circle pictures at the bottom of each page and if they can find them in the scene.
- Choose one of the scenes. Talk about the animals together and what they are like (e.g. *furry*, *scaly*, *big*, *small*), and where they live (e.g. *in the water*, *on the land* etc).
- As you look at the different scenes together, ask your child what they think it would feel like to be in each place? (e.g. *hot*, *cold*, *wet*, *icy*) Encourage your child to use words such as 'hotter', 'colder' etc to compare the different places.